For Reuben & all the other babies
R. I.

For Sophia, Zaki, Molly, Charlotte Rose & Baby Ivy
N. S.

Bloomsbury Publishing, London, Berlin, New York and Sydney

Hardback edition first published in Great Britain in May 2011 by Bloomsbury Publishing Plc
Paperback edition first published in Great Britain in August 2011 by Bloomsbury Publishing Plc

Bloomsbury Publishing Plc, 36 Soho Square, London, W1D 3QY

A CIP catalogue record of this book is available from the British Library

Hardback ISBN 978 1 4088 1118 4

1 3 5 7 9 10 8 6 4 2

Paperback ISBN 978 1 4088 0462 9

1 3 5 7 9 10 8 6 4 2

Printed in China by Toppan Leefung Printing Ltd, Dongguan, Guangdong

www.bloomsbury.com

Ten Little Babies

ROSE IMPEY

Illustrated by
NICOLA SMEE

BLOOMSBURY

LONDON BERLIN NEW YORK SYDNEY

Ten little babies on a sunny day.
Ten little babies left on the grass to play.

And if **one** little baby should start to

crawl away . . .

There'd be **nine** little babies left on the grass to play.

Nine little babies on a sunny day.
Nine little babies left on the grass to play.

And if **ONE** little baby should start to

float away . . .

There'd be **eight** little babies left on the grass to play.

Eight little babies on a sunny day.
Eight little babies left on the grass to play.

And if **one** little baby should start to

slide away . . .

There'd be seven little babies left on the grass to play.

Seven little babies on a sunny day.
Seven little babies left on the grass to play.

And if **one** little baby should start to

trot away . . .

There'd be SIX little babies left on the grass to play.

Six little babies on a sunny day.
Six little babies left on the grass to play.

And if **one** little baby should start to

sail away . . .

There'd be **five** little babies left on the grass to play.

Five little babies on a sunny day.
Five little babies left on the grass to play.

And if **one** little baby should start to

climb away . . .

There'd be **four** little babies left on the grass to play.

Four little babies on a sunny day.
Four little babies left on the grass to play.

And if **one** little baby should start to

zoom away . . .

There'd be three little babies left on the grass to play.

Three little babies on a sunny day.
Three little babies left on the grass to play.

And if ONE little baby should start to

hop away...

There'd be TWO little babies left on the grass to play.

TWO little babies on a sunny day.
TWO little babies left on the grass to play.

And if ONE little baby should start to

fly away . . .

There'd be ONE little baby left on the grass to play.

One little baby on a sunny day.
One little baby left on the grass to play.

And if **one** little baby should start to

hide away . . .

There'd be NO little babies left on the grass to play.

Ten little babies, where can they all be?
Ten little babies, shall we count and see?

One, two, three, four, five,
six, seven, eight, nine, ten.
Ten little babies collected up again.

Ten little babies, it's time they went to bed.
Ten little babies, little sleepyheads.

If we're very quiet . . . shhhh . . .
and no one makes a peep . . .

There'd be ten little babies all in their cots asleep.